NURSERY RHYMES

Illustrated
by
Maud
Humphrey

Derrydale Books
New York • Avenel, New Jersey

New Artwork
Copyright © 1992 by Outlet Book Company, Inc.
All rights reserved
First published in 1992 by Derrydale Books
distributed by Outlet Book Company, Inc.,
a Random House Company,
40 Engelhard Avenue
Avenel, New Jersey 07001

Manufactured in the United States

Cover design and special artwork by Clair Moritz

Library of Congress Cataloging-in-Publication Data
Nursery rhymes / illustrated by Maud Humphrey.
p.   cm.
Summary: Presents a collection of traditional rhymes accompanied
by Victorian illustrations.
ISBN 0-517-08274-8
1. Nursery rhymes.   2. Children's poetry.   [1. Nursery rhymes.]
I. Humphrey, Maud, b. 1868, ill.
PZ8.3.N9359   1992
398.8—dc20   92-13790
CIP
AC

8   7   6   5   4   3   2   1

Little Bo-Peep
      has lost her sheep,
And can't tell
      where to find them;
Leave them alone,
      and they'll come home,
Wagging their tails
      behind them.

Little Boy Blue,
   come blow your horn,
The sheep's in the meadow,
   the cow's in the corn!
Where is the little boy,
   minding his sheep?
He's under the haystack
   fast asleep!

Pussycat, pussycat,
    where have you been?
I've been to London
    to look at the Queen.

Pussycat, pussycat,
   what did you there?
I frightened a little mouse
   under the chair.

Curly locks! curly locks!
    wilt thou be mine?
Thou shalt not wash dishes,
    nor yet feed the swine;
But sit on a cushion
    and sew a fine seam,
And feast upon strawberries,
    sugar and cream!

Ding, dong, bell.
The cat's in the well!
Who put her in?
Little Johnny Green.

Who pulled her out?

Little Johnny Stout.

What a naughty boy was that

To drown poor pussycat.

Little Tommy Tucker,
sings for his supper.
What shall he sing for?
White bread and butter.
How shall he cut it
without any knife?
How will he marry
without any wife?

As Tommy Snooks and Betsey Brooks
Were walking out one Sunday,
Said Tommy Snooks to Betsey Brooks
Tomorrow will be Monday.

Little Nancy Etticote
In a white petticoat
With a red nose;
The longer she stands
The shorter she grows.

Lucy Locket lost her pocket.
Kitty Fisher found it;

There was not a penny in it,
But a ribbon 'round it.

Little Jack Horner
sat in a corner
Eating a Christmas pie.
He put in his thumb
and pulled out a plum
And said: "What a good boy am I!"

As I was going up Primrose Hill,
Primrose Hill was dirty.
There I met a pretty miss,
And she dropped me a curtsey.

When I was a bachelor,
　　I lived by myself,
And all the bread and cheese I got
　　I put upon the shelf.
The rats and the mice they made
　　such a strife,
I was forced to go to London,
　　to get myself a wife.
The streets were so broad,
　　and the lanes were so narrow,
I had to bring my wife home
　　on a wheelbarrow.

The wheelbarrow broke,
and my wife had a fall,
Down came wheelbarrow,
little wife and all.

Sing a song of sixpence,
A pocket full of rye,
Four and twenty blackbirds
Baked in a pie.
When the pie was opened
The birds began to sing—
Oh, wasn't that a dainty dish
To set before the king?

Hush-a-bye, baby,
on the tree top,
When the wind blows,
the cradle will rock;
When the bough breaks
the cradle will fall,
Down will come baby,
cradle and all.

Hot cross buns, hot cross buns
One a penny, two a penny,
Hot cross buns.
If your daughters don't like them,
Give them to your sons.
One a penny, two a penny,
Hot cross buns.

The North Wind doth blow,
and we shall have snow.
And what will poor Robin
do then
poor thing?
He will hop to the barn,
And to keep himself warm
Will hide his head under
his wing:
poor thing.

There was a little boy and a little girl
Lived in an alley;
Says the little boy to the little girl,
"Shall I, oh! shall I?"

Says the little girl to the little boy,
"What shall we do?"
Says the little boy to the little girl,
"I will kiss you."

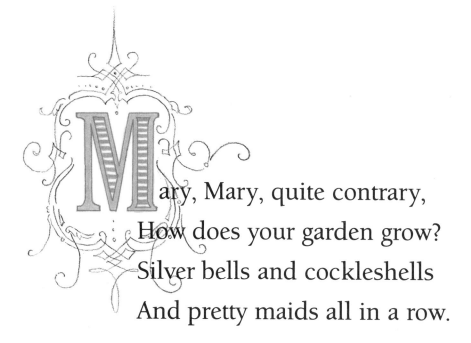

ary, Mary, quite contrary,
How does your garden grow?
Silver bells and cockleshells
And pretty maids all in a row.

Little Polly Flinders
Sat among the cinders,
Warming her pretty little toes!
Her mother came and caught her,
And whipped her little daughter,
For spoiling her nice new clothes.

Jack and Jill went up the hill,
To fetch a pail of water;
Jack fell down and broke his crown
And Jill came tumbling after!

Little Miss Muffet
sat on a tuffet,
   Eating some curds and whey;
Along came a spider
and sat down beside her,
   And frightened Miss Muffet away!

Bobby Shaftoe's gone to sea,
Silver buckles on his knee;
He'll come back and marry me,
Bonny Bobby Shaftoe!
Bobby Shaftoe's young and fair,
Combing down his yellow hair,
He's my love for evermore,
Bonny Bobby Shaftoe.